School of ROARS

Show and Tell

pat
a
Cake

When the stars come out
and it's night once more,
It's time to go to the School of Roars,
Wake up monsters and stretch your paws,
Jump up and go to the School of Roars!

It was another super-snufflesome night at the School of Roars.
The monsters were very excited. It was time for Show and Tell!

"Good roaring, monsters!" said Miss Grizzlesniff. "Did you all remember to bring in something special to show the class?"

"YES!"

growled the monsters.

Yummble went first. He waved his Guzzlespoon in the air. "I use it to guzzle up big gulps of slime!"

Icklewoo's Show and Tell sprang out of her pot. "This is my Snappy Plant!"

SNAP!

"What a lovely, friendly plant," said Miss Grizzlesniff.

"These are my Icky-Stickers!" giggled Meepa.

"Would you like to see my Giddy Glasses?" asked Wingston. "They change colour every time I blink!"

"And Wufflebump," said Miss Grizzlesniff, "have you got anything to show us?"

Wufflebump nodded. He had made some yummy Monster Biscuits for Show and Tell.

Wufflebump's biscuit tin started to rumble and shake
as he opened it. A creature leapt out!
"Where have my biscuits gone?" he wailed.

"Oh my claws!" cried Miss Grizzlesniff.
"This is my dog, Growlbert," gasped Wufflebump. "He must
have eaten all the biscuits!"

Miss Grizzlesniff had a good idea. "Can you tell us all about Growlbert instead?"
Wufflebump grinned.

"I got him when he was a puppy . . .

he loves digging . . .

he can sit,
stand and
howl . . .

. . . and he likes
burying Bunglebones!"

"Why don't you sit him down in the squishy corner?"
said Miss Grizzlesniff.

"Now class," said Miss Grizzlesniff, "I'd like you to write about your Show and Tell items. Off you go!"

The monsters got out their writing books. But when they ran to fetch their special things, they weren't there.

"My Snappy Plant!"

Everything had DISAPPEARED!

The monsters stamped their feet and shook their claws.
They were very cross and started to argue.

Miss Grizzlesniff got up from her desk.

"Class!" she said. "I can't hear when you all roar at once.
Please don't blame one another."

Everyone said sorry. "CUDDLES!"

The monsters decided to work together to solve the mystery of where their Show and Tell things had gone.

"Did anyone see or hear anything strange?" asked Miss Grizzlesniff.

"I heard stomping noises," said Wingston.

"And I saw a footprint," said Yummble. "Like those . . ."

Everyone looked down. There were lots of strange footprints on the floor!

"Follow those footprints!" squeaked Meepa.

The footprints led the monsters all the way to the squishy corner, where they found . . . "GROWLBERT!"

"I think he's been busy digging a big hole and burying treasure," said Miss Grizzlesniff.

The monsters looked down. All of their special things were at the bottom of Growlbert's hole!

Miss Grizzlesniff decided that Growlbert should go outside. She tried to open the classroom door.
"Oh my claws! The door handle has broken!" she shrieked.
"We're trapped!"

Growlbert wagged
his tail and started to
tunnel under the door.

When he got to the
other side, he stood
up and opened the
classroom door!

"Good boy," said Miss Grizzlesniff. "You deserve a gold star for your excellent digging skills."

"Look Growlbert, you're teacher's pet!" said Wufflebump.

Every little monster agreed that Growlbert was the best Show and Tell surprise ever.

THE END

LOOK AND FIND

It's amazing what friends can do. When the little monsters worked together, it was easy to find their special things.

Are you good at finding things? Take a closer look at the class. Can you find all of the little pictures hiding inside the big picture?

Point to every object that you see.

book

poster

paints

Brian

window